Poisonous Animals

Written by Brylee Gibson

Some animals can
be poisonous.

Look at this wasp.
It has a stinger.
The stinger is poisonous.

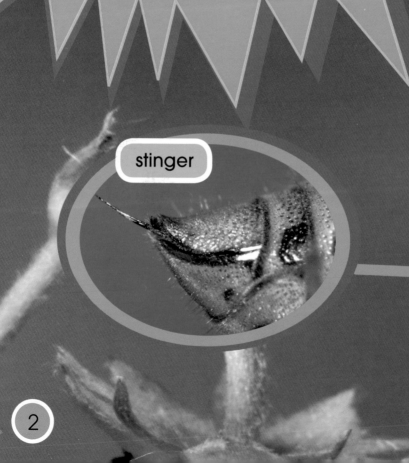

stinger

A scorpion has
a stinger.
The stinger is
on its tail.

stinger

A stingray has a stinger.
The stinger is on its tail, too.

The stingers are poisonous.

Look at this snake.
Look at its fangs.

The fangs are
inside its mouth.
They are poisonous.

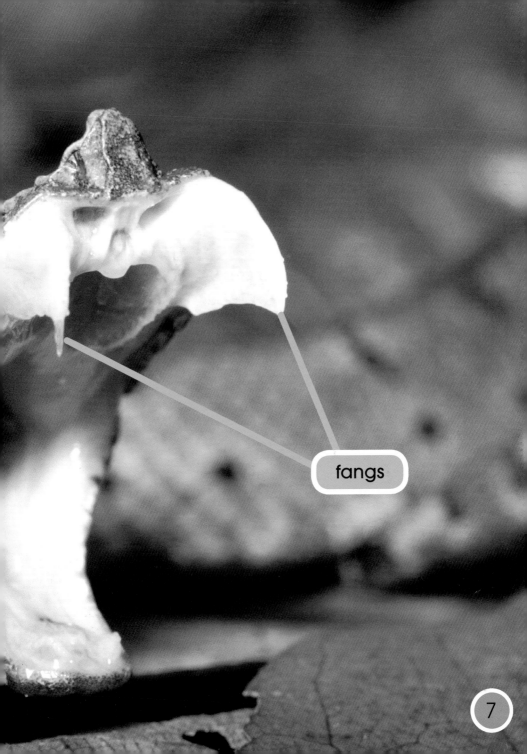

fangs

Look at this animal.
Look at its claws.

The claws are poisonous
on this animal.

claws

Look at this frog.
Look at the skin.

The skin on this frog
is poisonous.

skin

Look at this fish.
Some fish have spines.

The spines are
like needles.
The spines are poisonous.

spine

13

This is a fish, too.
It is poisonous.
The poison is inside the fish.

Index

Guide Notes

Title: Poisonous Animals
Stage: Early (2) – Yellow

Genre: Nonfiction
Approach: Guided Reading
Processes: Thinking Critically, Exploring Language, Processing Information
Written and Visual Focus: Photographs (static images), Index, Labels
Word Count: 122

THINKING CRITICALLY
(sample questions)
- Look at the title and read it to the children. Ask the children what they know about poisonous animals.
- Focus the children's attention on the index. Ask: "What are you going to find out about in this book?"
- If you want to find out about poisonous stingers, which pages would you look on?
- If you want to find out about poisonous spines, which page would you look on?
- Why do you think some animals might be poisonous?
- Which animal do you think might be very poisonous? Why?

EXPLORING LANGUAGE

Terminology
Title, cover, photographs, author, photographers

Vocabulary
Interest words: poisonous, stinger, wasp, stingray, scorpion, fangs, claws, skin
High-frequency word: inside
Positional words: on, inside

Print Conventions
Capital letter for sentence beginnings, periods, commas